# MELVIN
## Melvin's First Adventure

## JULES MORRIS

*Illustrated by Joshua Allen*

www.julesmorris.co.uk

*AuthorHouse™ UK*
*1663 Liberty Drive*
*Bloomington, IN 47403  USA*
*www.authorhouse.co.uk*
*Phone: 0800.197.4150*

*Published by AuthorHouse 11/07/2018*

*ISBN: 978-1-7283-8071-1 (sc)*
*ISBN: 978-1-7283-8070-4 (e)*

*Library of Congress Control Number: 2018913408*

*Print information available on the last page.*

authorHOUSE®

"Mum, can I have that toy train please?"

Mum: No.

"Ok, I tried...but I really want that."

"I know, I'll ask some of the 7 billion people on this planet for some money! 10p each should do it."

"Hi! Can I have some money please?"

Stranger: No.

(Again)
"Ok, but will you help me carry shopping?"

"Sure!"

"Why don't your kids help you with this?"

"Oh, I don't have any kids."

"If you'd like, I could help you
every time you go shopping"

"That's very kind, thank you! Here's one pound."

"Wow! I just started and I already have one £."

"Hi! Can I have some money please?"

Angry man: No.

"Why are you angry sir?"

"I don't like shopping."

"I can help you if you'd like?"

"Yes, here's a list and bring it to my house."

(Finishes)
"Here you go Mr."

(Angry man not so angry): "Thank you, I hate shopping! Here's a £."

"I can help you every week if you'd like?"

"Yes!"

"Ok, bye Mr."

Printed in the United States
By Bookmasters